ALLEN COUNTY PUBLIC LIBRARY
3 1833 05214 7320
FRIENDS
OF ACPL
APR 2 5 2007

Superfast Cars™

Corvette

Rebecca Hawley

PowerKiDS press.
New York

Published in 2007 by The Rosen Publishing Group, Inc.
29 East 21st Street, New York, NY 10010

Copyright © 2007 by The Rosen Publishing Group, Inc.

All rights reserved. No part of this book may be reproduced in any form without permission in writing from the publisher, except by a reviewer.

First Edition

Editor: Joanne Randolph
Book Design: Ginny Chu
Book Layout: Kate Laczynski
Photo Researcher: Sam Cha

Photo Credits: Cover, pp. 1, 4, 6, 10 © General Motors; pp. 8, 12 © www.shutterstock.com; p. 14 © Andre Duran/AFP/Getty Images; p. 16 © Alain Jocard/AFP/Getty Images; pp. 18, 20 © Getty Images.

Library of Congress Cataloging-in-Publication Data

Hawley, Rebecca.
Corvette / Rebecca Hawley. — 1st ed.
p. cm. — (Superfast cars)
Includes index.
ISBN-13: 978-1-4042-3643-1 (library binding)
ISBN-10: 1-4042-3643-0 (library binding)
1. Corvette automobile—Juvenile literature. I. Title. II. Series.

TL215.C6H39 2007
629.222'2—dc22

2006022355

Manufactured in the United States of America

Contents

Chevrolet makes the Corvette. Chevrolet is owned by General Motors.

An All-American

The first Corvette rolled out of the factory and into American driveways in 1953. At the time sports cars made in Italy and Germany were common. The Corvette was the first high-**performance**, superfast car to be made in America. The car has been an American **legend** ever since.

Corvettes put huge power and a low price together. This makes them different from their very costly European kin. Let's take a look at the Corvette.

Here is the 1953 Corvette Roadster. This was the first car made to drive well and look good, too.

The First Corvette

For a long time in America, no one cared what a car looked like. People just needed it to work.

In 1927, things changed. General Motors, which makes the Chevrolet Corvette, gave **designer** Harley Earl a job. Earl was the first person to try to make cars look better. He wanted to make a two-seat car to **compete** with the European sports cars that were brought to America. GM agreed, and Earl designed the 1953 Corvette.

The Corvette engine is small for how much power it gives the car. A driver just has to step on the gas and the engine is ready to spring into action.

Small Engine, Big Power

Corvette got a rocky start, and GM almost stopped making it. However, with a few changes to the **engine** the car soon became a top performer.

The Corvette's small, light engine gave the car a huge amount of power. Other sports cars had much more **complicated** engines. Corvette kept its engine simple but did not cut back on performance. In fact, Corvette's whole design had to do with keeping things simple.

The Corvette Stingray was one of the best-loved Corvettes of all time.

3 1833 05214 7326

Meet the Stingray

In 1963, GM made a Corvette **coupe**. The car was called a Stingray. The Stingray could reach 155 miles per hour (249 km/h).

This superfast car was a hit with car lovers. The Stingray held tightly to the road and went around corners smoothly. Drivers enjoyed the feeling of power from the engine. The fact that the car was easy to drive was a plus.

The C6 Z06 body is made out of lightweight aluminum instead of heavy steel. This car is the first one Chevrolet has made from something other than steel.

Meet the C6 Z06

In 2006, GM presented the C6 Z06. This Corvette has learned from the **decades** of Corvettes that have come before it. It is faster and more powerful, reaching 60 miles per hour (97 km/h) in just over 3 seconds. It is also beautiful to look at.

The engineers of the Z06 say they based this car on the Corvette race car, the C6-R. This is not hard to believe, since the Z06 can reach 198 miles per hour (319 km/h).

The C5-R is one of Corvette's race cars. It is based on the C5 road car but had some changes made to help it do well on the track.

On the Track

When a company makes a fast car, like a Corvette, it often wants to show off its **technology**. Many car companies make race cars as well as road cars. GM makes race-ready Corvettes, too.

Cars built for racing do not have to follow the same rules as those built for the road. This means they can be made to go faster. This is a good thing when you are trying to win a race!

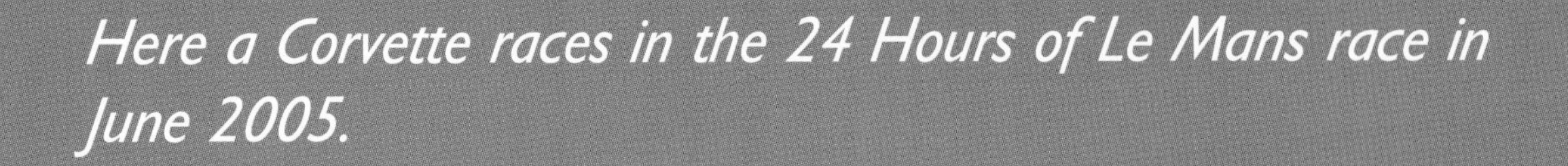
Here a Corvette races in the 24 Hours of Le Mans race in June 2005.

Winning Cars

Corvette has won a lot of **endurance** races with its race cars. The C5-R raced in the well-known 24 Hours of Le Mans race in France, the American Le Mans Series, and many other competitions. Between 2001 and 2006, it won many of these races.

The C6-R came out in 2005. It has won many races, too. In fact, it won every race it entered in the 2005 American Le Mans Series. It has been doing well ever since.

Corvette was the pace car for the Indianapolis 500 in May 2006.

Keeping Pace

In many track races, a pace car is used. This car is also called a safety car. It is sent out to slow down the race. This is done if there is an **accident**, bad weather, or something else that may put the drivers in danger.

The Indianapolis 500 picks a pace car each year. It is a great honor to be picked. Corvette has been picked as pace car for the Indy 500 eight times.

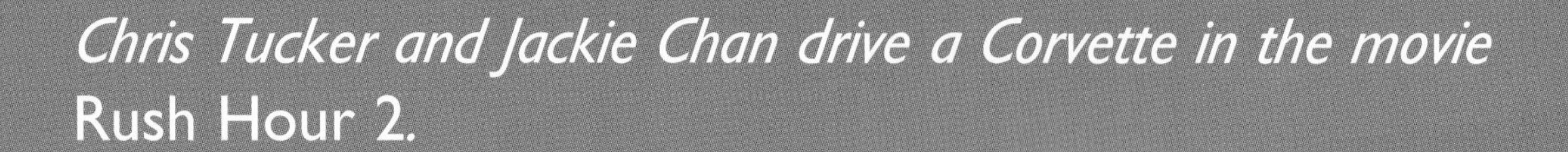

Chris Tucker and Jackie Chan drive a Corvette in the movie Rush Hour 2.

Pop Star

Corvette really is America's sports car. Corvette has become such a part of American **culture** that it shows up in the words to songs. Prince, Ja Rule, Pearl Jam, Aerosmith, Neil Young, and Rod Stewart are just a few of the bands who have talked about Corvettes in their music. Corvette has also starred in lots of movies, such as *Rush Hour* and *Rush Hour 2* with Chris Tucker and Jackie Chan. This is all in a day's work for the Corvette, though.

What Lies Ahead?

It is hard to imagine how Corvette can come up with a car that is better and faster than the C6 Z06. It sounds like Corvette is trying, though. It is said that soon Corvette will build a true supercar.

No one knows for sure what this supercar will be like. No one is sure how fast it will go, either. We do know that car lovers everywhere are looking forward to the next superfast Corvette.

Glossary

accident (AK-seh-dent) An unplanned and sometimes bad thing.

compete (kum-PEET) To go against another in a game.

complicated (KOM-pluh-kayt-ed) Hard to understand.

coupe (KOOP) A kind of car with two doors and a hard roof.

culture (KUL-chur) The beliefs, practices, and arts of a group of people.

decades (DEH-kaydz) Periods of 10 years.

designer (dih-ZYN-er) The person who makes the plan or the form of something.

endurance (en-DUR-ints) Strength and going a long way without getting tired easily.

engine (EN-jin) A machine inside a car or an airplane that makes the car or airplane move.

legend (LEH-jend) Something that has been famous and honored for a very long time.

performance (per-FOR-mens) The act of carrying out or doing.

technology (tek-NAH-luh-jee) The way that people do something using tools and the tools that they use.

Index

Web Sites

Due to the changing nature of Internet links, PowerKids Press has developed an online list of Web sites related to the subject of this book. This site is updated regularly. Please use this link to access the list:
www.powerkidslinks.com/sfc/corvette/